In Transylvania there's a town,
By name of Vampton-On-The-Down.
Above that town a castle sits,
With turrets, moat and pointy bits,
A castle guaranteed to make
Your spine go tingle, kneecaps quake.
For there lived two whose name's known far:
The Count and Countess Dracula.

The Count particularly tried
To keep the whole town scarified.
And being an expert you can tell,
He did his scaring *frightfully* well.
He'd bone-white hands with claw-like grips,
Hypnotic eyes, and blood-red lips,
Revealing, gleaming underneath:
The magic vampire FALSE FANG TEETH!

They frighten! They bite!
They come out at night!
The fangtastic adventures
Of Dracula's Dentures.

Chapter One: Count Dracula toddles off to the sea - alone.

One day the Count was in his bed,
When suddenly he woke and said:
"I'll see the sea!" So loudly that
His wife fell off the ceiling - splat!
"I've not played by the sea, nor made
A castle with my plastic spade,
For nearly half a century."
(That's fifty years to you and me).
"I'll leave at once!" he carried on,
"As soon as all the daylight's gone."
(For vampires hate the sizzling sun.)
His wife sang, "Seaside, here we come!"
But Dracula said, "No, my dear,
I'm sorry, you must stay right here
And keep 'em scared till I get back.
All righty? Good - I'm off to pack."

USBORNE RHYMING STORIES

THE FANGTASTIC ADVENTURES OF DRACULA'S DENTURES

Written by Philip Hawthorn

Illustrated by Kim Blundell

Designed by Non Figg

Edited by Jenny Tyler

The pictures in this book contain
A test to tax the biggest brain.
So scan each one with peeled-eye care,
Three vampire pets are hiding there.
That's Crafty Cat, Revolting Rat,
And not forgetting Belfry Bat.

For Theodore

He opened up his suitcase wide,
And wildly threw his things inside:
Some shirts and shorts and shiny shoes,
And trendy ties in reds and blues,
Silk underpants and satin vest -
"I have to be correctly dressed.
How cold d'you think it's going to be?
I'll take a sweater, maybe three."

"Now have we got some moon-tan lotion?
Don't worry, I'll mix up a potion.
I hope we don't get too much rain,
I think I'll go by scareoplane.
You seen my camera? Ah! My socks,
The denture fangs are in their box.
Oh help, is that the time? Must fly,
Have fun, my dear, kiss-kiss - goodbye!"

So Countess Drac was left to do
The scaring for a week or two.
Her head was full of creepy thoughts,
"I'll do a tour of all the haunts:
The graveyard, then the old folk's home,
They hate it when I moan and groan."
And then she had some inspiration,
Some wailing at the wailway station!

She rushed to get the false fang teeth,
But stopped and shrieked in disbelief...
They'd disappeared! Where could they be?
She started searching frantically.

6

She flung wide open cupboard doors,
Explored in all the chests of drawers.
She probed the wardrobe, turned each thing
Both inside out and outside in.
She scoured the bathroom, toilet too,
The playroom, dayroom, dining room.
She frisked Old Bram the cellar cat,
And all his fleas, in seconds flat.

From belfry high to dungeon low,
The C.D., T.V., video.
From here to there and all around,
(She dredged the moat and nearly drowned).
She looked in nooks and scanned the crannies,
And ransacked bedrooms, even Granny's.
She hunted hard from top to bottom,
Then sadly sighed, "I just ain't got 'em."

They frighten! They bite!
They've vanished from sight.
(But where have they gone?
You'll know later on.)
The fangtastic adventures
Of Dracula's dentures.

Chapter Two: Countess Drac finds scaring a fangless task.

"Oh well," she said, "I'll still depart,
 I've plenty other scary parts."
  With that, on wings of bat, she flew
   To 4, Magnolia Avenue.
   To give the children living there
   A nightmare frightmare spooky-scare.
  She screamed and howled, then in a trance
 She did her dreaded Deathly Dance.
But far from faces fraught with fear,
Each child just smiled from ear to ear.
"What's up?" she cried. "Why don't you shake?
    I'm Dracula, for goodness' sake."
    "You can't be," both the children sang,
   "Because you haven't any fangs.
Don't kid yourself, 'cause you're about
   As scary as a Brussels sprout."

The poor old Countess felt a fool,
"It weren't like this at training school."
And all that week, despite her trying,
She just could not be terrifying.
Folk said, "Oh, darlin', save your breath,
D'you think we fear being *gummed* to death?"
And then they laughed and threw her money,
A fangless vampire is quite funny.

And soon the Countess came to be
A bit of a celebrity.
A crowd would gather every night,
To clap and cheer in sheer delight,
And go, "Bravo!" and then, "Encore!"
(That's French, you understand, for "more".)

To tell the truth, this fanglessness
Caused Countess Drac much strain and stress.
But strangely she began to find
Her heart was turning quite...well...*kind*.
So Monday morning off she went
To find herself some employ-ment.
The woman in the office smiled,
"Now this is what we've got on file...(Deep breath)
Tinker, tailor, soldier, sailor,
Picture framer, lion tamer,
Driving trains, flying planes,
Climbing cranes and cleaning drains.
Butcher, baker, undertaker,
Quaker, raker, model maker,
Fire fighter, streetlight lighter,
Children's rhyming story writer.
Solitary secretary
Down at hairy Mary's dairy,
Figure skater, illustrator,
See you later alligator,
Fortune teller, jelly seller,
Pea-pod sheller, flower smeller,
Mayor, weigher, hip-hoorayer,
Pot plant sprayer, ping-pong player,
Sing-song singer, round a campfire,
What's the best thing for a vampire? Hmmmmm?"

The Countess said, "I'd like to be
More useful to society."
The woman grinned and said "Today
This job came in, starts right away."

They gave to her, to keep her warm,
A lovely yellow uniform.
The Countess said, "It's cool and neat
To help folks safely cross the street!"

They frighten! They bite!
But did they tonight?
The fangtastic adventures
Of Dracula's Dentures.

Now stories of her transformation
Spread far and wide across the nation.
From town to town to village green,
By word of mouth and fax machine,
Until the news was overheard
By Queen Doreen the thirty-third.
(A fine young woman, hale and hearty,
A must for any skiing party.)
She slapped her throne and yelled, "What ho!
Not been to Vampton - ought to go!
They did invite one, one refused,
By vampires we are not amused.

So write at once and ask them, 'Is it
Safe to pay a royal visit?'
Then having sent them ample warning,
We'll sail for Vampton in the morning.
With westward wind and swooshing sea,
We'll be there Friday, half-past three.
(Oh goody, just in time for tea.)"

BUT...
While Queen Doreen's large entourage
Was heading for the royal barge,
In Vampton it's a different story,
For things were far from hunky dory.

For all this time the town had been
Observed by something quite obscene:
A hungry monster, roaring threats,
As big as fifty jumbo jets.
With orange hair and tartan shorts,
A beard (in which his food got caught),
And smelly too, with breath so strong
He moved about in clouds of pong.
From coast to coast he'd boast and brag,
"My burps could make a mountain sag."
And as for further down below -
I'm sure you wouldn't want to know.

To see this creature stout and stinking,
You'd think he'd eat you soon as blinking.
But no! You see, he was without
A single tooth - they'd all dropped out.
He'd spied the leaving Dracula,
And thought, "I'll be a burg-ular!"
He'd swiped the fangs - and thereupon
The Countess found them good and gone.

14

The monster, now with fangs in place,
Then yelled to all the populace,
"We'll play a game which should be fun,
It's called, 'I eat you one by one!'
I'll go and fetch a knife and spoon,
And start tomorrow afternoon."
Then laughed a wicked laugh, because
That's what the baddy always does.

They frighten! They bite!
With monster-ous might!
The fangtastic adventures
Of Dracula's dentures.

The next day, Friday, Drac got back,
And said, "Now for a scare attack!
I missed them badly while away,
Now where d'you put the fangs then, eh?"
The poor Countess could take no more,
And flung herself upon the floor.
She bawled and blubbered loud and long,
At this the Count said, "Something wrong?"

"Oh waah!" she wailed and then confessed:
The fangs, her job and all the rest -
The monster, who would soon begin
To crunch their bones and chew their skin.
Then Drac was angry, Drac was speechless,
His mouth wide open, eyes like peaches,
At last he said with bitter sigh,
"You got a *job?* I want to die!"

His wife yelled, "Listen, peanut brain,
Just let me spell it out again,
I know it's hard to comprehend,
But now the people are my friends.
And also - agh! I didn't say,
The royal party's due today!
I won't stand by and see the Queen
Get eaten like a tangerine."

Drac thought, then said, "Before we met,
I knew a witch called Antoinette.
She made my teeth from magic plastic,
To make my frightening quite fang-tastic.
Then, just in case they came to be
Some evil monster's property,
She gave to me a spell alarm,
To make them safe from doing harm.
To save the town we'll use this spell,
I'll get my dentures back, as well."

"But where's it hid?" the Countess cried,
The vampire glanced from side to side:
"I think it's in a dusty book,
Entrusted to our crusty cook.
It's thrust upon a rusty hook."
And thus discussed he rushed to look.

Drac soon got back and held aloft
A book as old as clouds are soft,
Then from it fell an envelope,
    He picked it up with rising hope.
        And on the back had been inscribed
            The spell that he had just described.
                "It's here!" he said. "Gosh! How exciting.
                    Oh help, it's all in joined-up writing."

His wife then grabbed it, "Give it here!
You nincompoop, it's all quite clear."
And then with no analysis
She yelled the spell, which went like this:

"Cosmic cola, magic molar - monster non corruptus.
Smite the frighter, fight the biter - fangus interruptus."

"I wonder if it's worked?" said Drac.
At once there was a thunder crack.
Forked lightning flashed and crashed around,
And rumbly wobbles shook the ground.
Through battered windows blizzards blew,
With eerie noises, such as 'wooo!'
And when it stopped, the Count said "Phew!
I think that's done the trick, don't you?"

The Countess ran without delay,
And told the people, "It's O.K!"
They gaily started preparations,
For royal welcome celebrations.
With blue balloons and new festoons,
And band to bash out brassy tunes.
The Mayor (who had a tiresome passion
For using language quite old-fashioned),
Cried, "Verily, this day will be
A pageant fit for royalty!
Ye worthy place in history!
Dear me, it's nearly half-past three."

Then trumpets fanfared, flags were flapped,
The waiting, happy crowd all clapped.
For everyone had looked and seen
The limousine of Queen Doreen.
Then out she stepped in purple gown,
With dazzling ceremonial crown,
And smiled and royal-waved amidst
The tons of flowers brought by kids.

Then suddenly disaster dawned,
In gobbly, smelly monster form.
He licked his lips with greedy grin,
With dribble drooling down his chin.
He looked toward the Queen and said,
"I think I'll start with sparkly head."
But just as Vampton went berserk,
The magic spell began to work.

The fangs flew from the monster's gums,
And promptly bit off both his thumbs.
They then proceeded to devour
The whole great beast in half an hour.
The crowd hurrahed with all their might
And yelled, "Ha-ha! It serves you right!"
They all adored the dentures' skill;
The score: Fangs won, the monster, nil.

They frighten! They bite!
They worked out all right!
The fangtastic adventures
Of Dracula's Dentures.

Chapter Five: What happened after the monster had munched itself.

While all the town then partied on,
The vampires argued all night long.
The cause of their ferocious fights
Was: should they still give Vampton frights?
The Count insisted they persist,
The Countess wished that they desist.
At length they compromised and planned
To build a theme park, Vampireland.

GHOST TRAIN

HIDE & SEEK

Inside, each ride was well designed
To make for quite a frightening time.
THE VAMPIRE CASTLE, CREEPY CREEK,
THE GRUESOME GRAVEYARD, HIDE AND SHRIEK.
The GHOST TRAIN gave the greatest fear,
For Drac could make real ghosts appear.
And there were always screaming sounds
Escaping from the BAT-GO-ROUND.

This meant the venture, more or less,
Became an overnight success.

Three cheers for Vampireland, for sending
Everyone a happy ending.

For Vampton, fear had been destroyed,
And all the people now enjoyed
A thriving tourist industry,
(The Queen was seen there frequently).

The Count was thrilled, being highly paid
For making visitors afraid.

The Countess was, from its creation,
The brains behind the operation.
She crowned her newly found career
By selling denture souvenirs.
Her advertising on the door,
I think you may have heard before:

They frighten! They bite!
They come out at night!
They're ever so white!
Just wear them, you might...
Have fangtastic adventures
With Dracula's Dentures.